Paula Giuffrida is a debut writer who grew up in the city of Massachusetts. From an early age she has long enjoyed writing little stories, every now and then sending an article of interest to her local newspaper in New Hampshire. A strong imagination and love of writing guides in her words and thoughts. She enjoys comedy, family, and mystery books.

Paula Giuffrida

Jackson's Harmonica

AUSTIN MACAULEY PUBLISHERS®

LONDON • CAMBRIDGE • NEW YORK • SHARJAH

Ordering Information
Quantity sales: Special discounts are available on quantity purchases by corporations, associations, and others. For details, contact the publisher at the address below.

Publisher's Cataloging-in-Publication data
Giuffrida, Paula
Jackson's Harmonica

ISBN 9798891550780 (Paperback)
ISBN 9798891550797 (ePub e-book)

Library of Congress Control Number: 2024908823

www.austinmacauley.com/us

First Published 2024
Austin Macauley Publishers LLC
40 Wall Street, 33rd Floor, Suite 3302
New York, NY 10005
USA

mail-usa@austinmacauley.com
+1 (646) 5125767

20240817

To Jackson,
In memory of Nanno,
Chet Giuffrida.

A special thank you to Jeffery Paolino for his helpful illustration
and ideas.

I was happy about graduating grade school, but feeling a little down about leaving a few friends I made. The sadness left me pretty fast when I thought about going to Marigold High School.

Tom, Audrey, Mike and Sammy were my friends.

We always hung together. I considered them my best friends.

When I was about 10 years old, my parents bought me a drum set for my birthday. At that age, I just banged away in my room and gave them a headache. I loved banging away and was determined to conquer the rhythm, which, of course never came to be. Finally, after a few weeks of giving my parents more pounding and causing TV disruption, my dad sent me for drum lessons at the Fontain Music School. Twice a week. It was great. My drum instructor, Danny Morrelly, was great. He taught me all kinds of neat wrist action, foot techniques, rudiments and so much more. I was lovin' every minute.

My buddy, Mike, lived a few houses down from me and he messed around with his guitar. We would get together for a while in my room and just have a good time making up songs and tunes. One afternoon, my mom came in with a dish of chocolate chip cookies. With her warm smile, she remarked at our musical mess. "You guys are sounding pretty good." I turned towards Mike to see the same surprised look on his face.

"Really, Mom! You think!" I said.

"Yep, I do," she answered as she placed the cookies down on the table and walked out of the room.

Her approval grabbed hold in my head and stuck with me.

On one of our music messes before we were going to meet up with Tom, Audrey and Sammy at our usual haunt, Pizza Pan, I asked Mike what he thought about putting a band together. He didn't answer and just stood quiet. I continued on with my suggestion to try and convince him.

"It'll be a load of fun, Mike, really. Rehearsing together and picking out songs to play. And Audrey, too. She does piano. We could ask her to join in. C'mon. How about it?" I put my sticks down hoping for a good answer.

Mike looked down slowly at the floor and said, softly, "Cheez, Jack. We're just kids. By the time we make a band and put music together, we might all be old people and hate each other."

I laughed out loud. "Not gonna happen, no way!" I said.

Mike had more to say about it.

"How about Tom and Sammy? They don't play anything." I thought about what Mike had just said.

"Yaa, you're right Mike. Tom...hmmmm... Tom...I've got it! Tom is very good at putting things together. How 'bout we make him arrange everything for us, like an agent."

My head swelled up with ideas. On I went.

"And, Sammy...Sammy loves clothes, right? He can be our clothes designer. Put toughener what we will wear!"

As I shook my head with amazing approval, Mike still did not buy into it.

"I don't know, Jack. I've got to think about it." I was not liking his decision but I accepted it.

"OK, well, let's go to Pizza Pan," I said sadly.

It was only one week away from Marigold High. I was nervous thinking about it.

I gave Audrey and Sammy a call to come over to my place.

And then I called Tom. I knew that Mike was on his way. I decided to talk to all of them about forming my band, hoping to convince them.

Mom greeted everyone as they arrived.

"Hi," she said. "What brings you guys here today?" she asked.

Sammy answered, "Dun no. Jack called and said to come over."

"Oh, OK..." Mom replied. "I'll come up in a few with some sodas."

Audrey thanked her and they headed up the stairs.

I was sitting at my drum set when they came into the room. Mike took out his guitar and sat in the brown recliner tucked away in the corner next to my bureau dresser.

Tommy kinda embraced the mood. He got the talk going. "Heeyyy...this is nice, huh? Together. Like being at Pizza Pan, without the Pizza."

"Yeah, cool." Audrey said as she and Tommy sat on the bed and began to arm wrestle. A few seconds passed and Audrey yelled out. "No... oh no, Tommy, you're not doin' it."

Tommy just laughed out loud and remarked, "Too bad...I won! You're just too scrawny, Audrey," he said. But that wasn't enough for Tommy so he went on. "Next time we'll just flip coins, OK? That should be easy for ya." And he continued to laugh.

Audrey then gave him such a hard kick he rolled off the bed and onto the floor, but still kept laughing.

"Are you two all done, now?" Sammy said as he turned to Jack. "Let's get to it, Jack. What's up?"

Tommy stood up and Audrey gave him a quick smile. "I talked to Mike about us starting a band. What ya think?"

Audrey was first to speak up.

"A band? We're kinda like young, aren't we, Jack?"

Jack remembered hearing those same words from Mike.

He needed to change their minds.

"Nawww. C'mon, we can do it. We'll be in high school next week. High school, guys, freshmen...!

C'mon." I knew they needed to hear more so I continued my speech. "Me and Mike play pretty good together. And you, Audrey, you do piano. Right? You're our keyboard player."

I could see that Audrey's eyes opened wide. She answered with a huge grin, "Yeah, yeah! Count me in!" Mike stayed quiet and just strummed on his guitar.

Sammy took a small step towards the bed and replied, "Sounds like a good idea. Me and Tommy will watch and listen every time you get together, if that's OK with you ?"

Jack looked over at Mike, hoping he would remember his idea about including Sammy and Tommy. I turned to Sammy and Tommy.

"Tommy," I said "...you are great at putting things together and making them come out right... so you could be the one to put us on the right track... like an agent... OK?"

Tommy seemed surprised, and answered quickly, "Agent? You mean like a...go and fix it kinda guy?"

I further explained, "Ya...you set us up with a play date and make sure all is cool."

Tommy liked it. "OK...I'll do that..." he answered.

"And Sammy," I said as I stood close to him. "You're always fussing' with your clothes. You're a constant like my outfit?" I made a gesture pointing to his own colorful shirt.

He frowned, but smirked.

"You can design what we will wear and make us look really spiffy! How's that grab ya?"

Sammy gave a weird kind of grin, and then a big smile. I took that smile as a yes.

After a few seconds of absolute silence, Mike stood up straight and tall and gave off a heck of a yell.

"Let's do it! Let's do it!"

I was overtaken with unbelievable anticipation of what was to happen next.

After they left the room, I did not let one moment go by. I rushed downstairs and waited in the den for my dad to come home from work. I heard the car pull in the driveway.

As soon as he came in, I ran up and greeted him.

"Hey, Dad, can I talk with you?" I asked.

He seemed to notice my nervous approach.

"Ya, OK, Jack. Give me a minute."

I went back in the den. A few minutes later he came in.

"What's up, son?" he asked.

I gave him my idea about the band and asked if we could rehearse in the garage. I figured I'd better add a little sugar. "We will be careful, Dad, honest. Won't wreck anything."

I looked at him shyly as he put back his head and nodded.

"OK," he said. "But your school work comes first. A few times a week, that's it...OK?"

I couldn't have been happier at that moment. "Ya...yes...OK...thanks, Dad."

We all agreed to rehearse Tuesdays and Thursdays after school for just an hour or so and Sunday afternoon from 2 to 4. Marigold High School took some getting used to. Finding classes, new teachers, new kids, some strange, some nice, and some not so nice. But it all came together just fine.

And so did our rehearsals.

It was just me, Mike and Audrey at first, but on one afternoon in the cafeteria, Audrey spotted a boy she was friendly with from one of her classes having lunch by himself.

She decided to go over and join him. After a short while, she brought him over. "This is Peter," she said. "Peter Enstall."

"Guess what, Jack. Peter plays electric guitar."

Peter sat down and asked me if he could join up.

"Let me try out with you guys," he said.

Audrey stared with her usual wide eyes showing me her crossed fingers.

"I guess it would be OK..." I told him.

Audrey then chimed in. "Great! I'll bring Pete with me tomorrow."

Mike did not have the same lunch hour as

we did. I became worried about how he would welcome another guitar. Especially an electric one.

It was Tuesday. Mike and I were setting things up in the garage. Audrey came in with Peter.

She introduced him to Mike.

"Mike, meet Peter. He plays electric guitar and wants to try out with us."

Mike just looked over to me and shrugged his shoulders.

"Ok with me," he said.

Peter hooked up his guitar to the sound system he had brought and took a place next to Mike. We all began to play a familiar tune we all knew well.

After a few minutes into the tune, I could see that Mike was getting along with him. The next tryout was a little different. Mike waved his hand and stopped us from playing. He turned to Peter.

"Ahhhhh. Pete...I had the intro into this one... OK?" Pete raised up his guitar towards the ceiling.

"Yesss sir, Mr. Mike...I got it...!" He then bowed to Mike.

After that, they got along better than before. Our new manager, Tommy, dubbed us "FACES

IN TIME." Sammy set up our outfits, which were pretty much easy to get. A white T-shirt with a huge smiley faced clock, black pants tapered tightly at the bottom and our own brightly colored sneakers. All put together, it was a cool look.

One night after dinner, I went into my closet for a jacket. I spotted a box on the shelf tucked away in the back that had been there for a long time. I took it down and opened it up. It had toys inside. A whistle, a small train, a worn-out teddy bear, some cards, puzzles and other kid stuff. I was about to close it up when I saw something shiny. I reached in and pulled out this brand-new shiny silver harmonica with diamond shaped carvings along the sides. It was not a toy. I tried to play it.

The sound was very soothing and different. I needed to know more about it.

Mom and Dad were watching the Westminster Best of Show Dogs. Our dog, Ollie, a lovable beagle, was lying next to Dad. I showed them this harmonica and asked, "When did I get this? I found it in my toy box." Dad looked over to my mom and smiled.

Mom began to tell me about it.

"Hmmm, I think you were 9. The whole world was hit hard with a deadly virus. Everyone was confined to their homes. If and when you did go out, you were required to wear masks. We all had to get vaccinated. It was a terrible time. So...being cooped up for such a long time, Dad got you this harmonica just to keep you busy. He used to play one and thought you might like it."

Then Dad chimed in, "You should have seen yourself..." he said laughing... "trying to play it...you were drooling...like Ollie when she eats too fast..." Mom laughed and went on with her story. "When you got bored with it, we put it away in your toy box."

"Trying it out again?" Dad asked.

"Nahhh...I was just curious about it," I answered.

At our next rehearsal, I took out the harmonica and started to play into it along with the tune we were putting together. It didn't go over well.

"What's goin' down?" said Mike. Is that a harmonica? he asked.

Peter just smirked a little.

Audrey liked it. She responded.

"Hey...that's a really nice one...I know a girl who plays one. It's great! A cool piece."

Sammy knew something more about it and he gave his own opinion. "Yeah," he said. "You gotta hear Stevie Wonder play it.

Fantastic! and Bob Dylan, and Steven Tyler and goin' way back there was Little Walter..."

Jack was taken back by all this info and interrupted Sammy.

"Wow, Sammy! How come ya know so much about a harmonica?" he asked.

Sammy replied, "My dad played one when he was with this Western outfit. He was terrific at it. I learned a lot from him." Jack took the harmonica and put it into his back pocket. We continued on with rehearsal and we were sounding pretty darn good.

It was pouring rain. It came down hard and heavy. I went into the garage to cover my drum set. As I turned to shut the garage doors, I spotted a little girl standing at the very end of the driveway holding an umbrella. She just stood there, in the pouring rain, staring out towards the garage. I was about to go out and see if she needed help with something, but she was gone.

"Jack," my mom yelled out to me from the bottom of the stairs. "Your cell phone is beeping." I quickly ran down and picked it up.

It was Sammy... "Yeah, Sammy," I said, "what's up?" He answered me with a kinda nervous voice.

"Tommy called me! Get this one!" he said.

"He wants you guys to play at his parents' 15th anniversary at the King's Table restaurant! He's gonna call you!" Those words sent a cold chill through my body, but I managed to answer him.

"Holy crap! You are kidding, right? You're kidding!"

Tommy replied, again nervously...

"Uh...uhhhh...nope, no way...I'm not!"

When I shut the cell, I sat on the sofa, dumfounded, waiting for Tommy to call.

Within minutes, it beeped.

"Jack, I got a big one for ya!" he said.

I interrupted him. "Ya, I know...Sammy just called."

"Oh, he did...He spoiled my big surprise," Tommy replied.

I didn't wait one second to answer him.

"Surprise? Tommy? Are you nuts! We can't do a party like that. We're not ready!" I said with a harsh firm tone.

I wasn't expecting the feedback I got from Tommy.

"Huh? C'mon Jack! You guys are doin' great! This party isn't until September the 19th. That's plenty of time to put a few tunes together. Jack... it'll be such a treat!"

"Oh...sure it will, Tommy. It will be a treat all right!" I said. "Thank your parents, but tell them we're not ready to do that. OK?" I answered with a slightly sad tone.

Tommy was not having any of my remarks.

"Oh...no, Jack. no...I'm not gonna tell them that. No way! My dad can't wait for this party with you performing! Please, Jack you can do this! You can...!"

I couldn't resist Tommy's pleading.

"Cheeeezzzz! Ya, ya...OK...You had better hope and pray we can pull this off and not make fools of ourselves, Tommy!"

After I hung up from the jolting phone call, I desperately needed to talk to my dad. When he got home from work, I gave him some time to settle down and talk with Mom for a bit. Then, I joined up with him while he was resting and reading the paper. I sat down on the chair. He peered out from the paper.

"Hey, Jack," he said. "How's it all going?"

I answered right away. "I'm worried sick, Dad." He put down his paper and curled his lip.

"What's wrong?" he asked.

"Well..." I started to say. "See...ahhh...Tommy's parents are having a 15-year anniversary party."

Dad replied. "I know, your mom mentioned it."

I went on with my scary story. At least to me it was.

"Ya, OK...well...see...Tommy's parents want us to play at the Kings Table for that party and... well...geeezzz Dad, we're not ready for that yet. I tried to tell Tommy but he wouldn't listen. I don't know what to do."

I looked into my dad's eyes, praying for a solution.

He had one.

"OK...Jack, just calm done and think this through. When is the party?"

"About 4 months away. September 19th," I said.

Dad nodded a few times and answered with a confident and reassuring voice.

"That seems like a good enough stretch for you guys to put a few numbers together. Something easy like soft tunes and maybe one rock song. Your mom is good with knowing music tunes. She can help. You'll only need about 3 or 4 numbers... that's all...And besides, Tommy's parents know you're not professionals. They just want to hear you play."

"I'm sure you can do it. You might have to include another day or so of practice, but you can handle it. I say go for it!" Dad's words filled me up with encouragement. He gave me a huge lift up.

We were all together in the garage. The first rehearsal for this party. My mom helped me pick our first number. An old classic by Sinatra called The Best Is Yet To Come.

I gave out a quick beat to begin. After a few seconds or so, Mike stopped playing and said firmly to me, "You're losing the beat Jaaaaaaacccccckson! It's too slow..."

he said. I didn't mind being criticized, but I wanted to save the embarrassment and give some back.

"Maybe you're rushing it, Miiiiiiiccccchhhelllll."

I screamed and put down my sticks.

Just then Audrey got up and went over to Mike. She slapped him behind his head. "Knock it off, you guys!"

Peter said nothing, but then, he never did. He would not complain about anything. Just loved to play.

"OK...ya...OK...sorry," Mike muttered. "I'm cranked up is all." We all at that very moment yelled out, "ONE MORE TIME!" June 8th, one awfully hot day. About 87 and climbing. The garage door was open and we all started to set up for practice. Sammy and Tommy were just coming in when Sammy asked if anybody knew who the girl was standing at the end of the driveway.

I ran over, wondering if it was the same girl I had seen on that day it was pouring rain. It was her.

"Yeah," I said. "She was here once before. I don't know who she is."

Audrey came to have a look. "That's my neighbor, Amy...Amy Dawson," she said. "I told her about our band. She must have walked here."

Peter and Mike both offered their opinion.

"I think we should invite her in. She probably just wants to listen to us rehearse. No big deal about it."

Audrey had a very different response. "I don't know guys. Amy is very, very shy. I mean…well… she can't speak very clearly. She stutters lots. Might be she has autism. When she gets afraid of anything she goes out of control and cries."

We can deal with it, right Jack?" Peter said.

Jack looked out at this little girl and agreed with Peter.

"OK…Audrey, you go get her."

Audrey replied. "OK, but if she gets jittery or scared, I'll have to leave and take her home."

"Sure, OK…go get her," Jack said.

Amy pranced into our garage with Audrey. She was waving her hand all around at us and had this wonderful big smile.

We could almost see the shyness in her pretty brown eyes. She was the cutest little girl. It was love at first sight for us all.

Audrey took her hand and introduced us to her one at a time. "This is Peter, Amy. And this is Mike…This guy over here is Jack." Over to the corner she went with Amy.

"This is Sammy…and this one is Tommy." All through the intro's Amy kept on waving and smiling. She was awesome. Audrey took her over to my mom's old lawn chair and sat her down next to Sammy.

"How old is she, Audrey?" Sammy asked.

Audrey replied, "I think 9 or 10...not sure."

Amy looked at Sammy, still with a big smile. "I'mmmmm tttttennn..." she said.

We got ourselves together and started playing. Amy just sat and listened. On the next number, she stood up and clapped and laughed. Tommy went over to her and dubbed her the very first fan of "FACES IN TIME." We all adored her.

We finally managed to complete two numbers. Still two more to go. It was now into late July. September wasn't far off.

July 20. Not every rehearsal went smoothly. This was one of them. It was the first time Peter became upset and angry. "Cripes!" he screamed out. "This number is horrid! We sound like a pack of wolves or something! I'm gonna unplug my guitar and get the hell out of here!"

Peter didn't realize that his high-pitched anger frightened Amy.

She put her hands up to her face and screamed out, "Noooooo...nooo...no!" She then reached into her small purse she always carried and pulled out this small, chrome harmonica that was all dented on each side and began to play. We were all amazed at how terrific it sounded! It calmed her right down. When she finished, she sat back down and waved and smiled, like she always did.

"Holy cow! Jack said...that was wild!"

"Yep...remember, Jack..." Audrey remarked. "I told you about the girl I knew who played harmonica."

"Oh...ya...I remember," he said. "I'll be right back, guys."

Peter then felt bad about losing it. He went over to Amy. "Sorry, princess...didn't mean to scare you," he said.

Amy looked up at him with that glorious smile. "Oookkkayyy, Peter...okayyy."

Peter just melted away by her big brown eyes.

A few minutes later, Jack came back. He went over to Amy and handed her the shiny new harmonica he had found in his toy box. Her eyes lit up. Her smile became wider. She immediately began playing it. All of us stood quietly and just listened to the amazing sounds coming from this little instrument. She played it beautifully. She had the same passion for music we all had and it came pouring out of that harmonica. When she was done playing, she reached over to give the harmonica back.

"It's yours, Amy...you keep it," Jack told her.

She gave Jack a big hug. "Thankkkk you, Jaaacck." Following the surprise from Amy, Jack agreed with Peter the song was not good enough. They agreed to scrap it for another one that Tommy said his parents loved. It was sung by Natalie Cole called "This Will Be." They got to work on it right away.

August 10th. With three songs completed, FACES IN TIME was feeling pretty good. September 19th was not very far away. Tommy set up the songs in the order he felt they should be played. He presented his listing with confidence.

"We open up with Sinatra's 'The Best Is Yet To Come'. Next, 'This Will Be' and the third, Kenny Rogers, 'Through the Years'. Is that a go?" he asked.

They all agreed it was a great set-up. They still needed one more song, just one more.

Thursday, August 15th. While clowning around in the garage before the rehearsal got started, Mike was feeling a funny side. "Hey," he remarked loudly, "we are FACES IN TIME, right?"

All gave a nod and Sammy said, "Ya...and so?"

Mike laughed. "Well, I was thinkin' of the initials, F I T. 'Fit', we are Fit. Get it! Fit. There was an old dusty pillow next to Amy; she picked it up and while laughing out loud, threw it at Mike. Mike formed a fist toward Amy, but she ignored that and kept on laughing. It was a moment they would not forget."

Jack was watching an old McHale's Navy TV show with Ollie lying at his feet. His mom came over with a piece of apple pie. "Just for you," she said as she handed it over. She sat next to him and asked, "Is the band all ready? It's getting close to the date. Dad has snuck around the garage a few times to listen. He told me he liked what he heard."

Jack smiled and answered. "I knew he was there. He's my rock."

Mom continued asking, "Are you done now?"

Jack shook his head and replied sadly, "Naw... not yet. We still have one more song to do. We're back and forth with what to close with, but come up with nothing." Jack's mother could sense the low from him.

"Mind if I make a suggestion?" she asked.

"Sure, I'm all ears...go ahead, shoot."

Mom was eager and ready as she turned to him and said, "Well, I was listening to the Rockin' all night radio station and they played a number that I thought would be a great last song for the band."

Jack patted Ollie and replied, "OK...what was it?"

"It was called Everything I Do, I Do It For You," she said. Jack straightened up on the sofa. He knew the song.

"Yes! Ya...Mom...you're the greatest!" he said to her as he kissed her on the cheek. He left the room and called up the band for a special rehearsal tomorrow afternoon.

When they all arrived, Mike asked, "What's so important?"

Jack answered with excitement in his tone.

"I've got the last number and I think it's a winner!"

"Good..." Audrey blurted out... "spit it out."

Jack stood and looked at FACES IN TIME, hoping this was the song to close with.

"It's called Everything I Do," he said as he waited for an approval.

Peter was first to speak up. "I know that one... Yeah...Yeah...good one to close with...I like it...I like it a lot," he said. Mike and Audrey nodded their heads and gave a thumbs up.

Sammy agreed. Tommy had a different approach to it.

"Ahhh...one thing about it...It needs a singer," he said.

Jack answered abruptly. "Huh? Tommy, where are we gonna get a vocalist!" Suddenly there was a loud strumming from Peter's guitar.

Instantly, to all of their immediate shock, Peter's voice filled the garage air.

"I'd like to do it...I have a decent voice and I can hold a tune pretty darn good."

Mike tuned in. "Hooop dee doo dahhh! We've got a singer!"

Time quickly passed by. It was now September 8th.

We were setting up rehearsal again for the last song, Everything I Do, figuring when it's completed, the rest of the time we will rehearse all the songs again.

There was just enough time to wrap it all up before the 19th.

This was Tuesday afternoon, around 3, right after school, when Audrey came in with a worried look on her face.

We all noticed Amy was not with her.

She quickly went over to Jack. "Jack, I need to ask you something important," she said.

"Ya...what's up? Is Amy OK?" he asked concerned.

Audrey nodded and said, "She's good...but...well, you know she loves us, right?" By this time Jack got nervous.

Mike and Peter saw something was wrong and went over to them.

Mike asked, "What's goin' on? Where's Amy?"

"That's what Audrey is about to tell us," Jack replied. Sammy and Tommy stayed in their corner of the garage not showing too much concern for what was happening. Audrey began explaining.

"OK...well. Ahhh...see...Amy asked me to ask you guys if she could play her new harmonica for the last song...at the party! She stayed home to practice it."

A few seconds of total disbelief and finally Jack spoke up.

"Good God, Audrey...now!? Now!? We don't have time to fit her in...Oh...Jeez!"

"I know, Jack, I know, but I just didn't know what to say to her," Audrey said while almost coming to tears.

Mike and Peter stayed silent, until Mike gave a look over to Peter and said while moving his head from side to side. "Why don't we give her a chance? We know she plays a super harmonica.

Why not? We still have more than a week left... We can squeeze in a few more rehearsals."

Peter agreed and added, "It's only one song."

Jack then yelled over to Tommy. "Hey, manager, Amy wants to join in and play with us."

Tommy came over with Sammy. "Wow!" Tommy replied.

"Cutting it really tight, huh? Let her try. Won't hurt."

Sammy also had his say. "Sure, why not let her try. She's been with us from day one, right? So she knows every song, every note. Right? She knows our music setup as well as we do, maybe better," he said with a smile.

Jack wasn't sure. "Playing by yourself and playing with a band is a lot different, but..."

Jack turned to Audrey. "Tell her it's OK."

Sammy gave out a huge, "Yes. If she plays with us, I have the perfect outfit for her!"

Audrey added with a doubtful look, "What if she doesn't cut it? She might freak out and lose it. Start crying or carrying on or something."

"I'll take care of her if that should happen," Sammy answered. "Besides, she like me the best."

Faces called a rehearsal for the very next day, September 9th. They all knew this was going to be the most difficult one they ever had, with Amy and her harmonica.

It was about 2:45. Audrey came into the garage with Amy. Mike was already strumming away and

Peter was plugging in and setting up. I sat at my drum set and just looked over at Audrey. We had already asked Audrey to give Amy direction and to watch her lead in. Sammy stood by the garage door. Tommy had not yet arrived. A few minutes and they were all ready to go. Audrey started to direct Amy.

"OK, now, Amy...don't be nervous, just play and have fun...You've been practicing the song and you know it...Watch me and when I point to you, start to play from the beginning. OK?" Amy answered with a big smile...

"Yaaaaa...I pracccticed a llllot."

"Good, now just watch me," Audrey said.

Amy held her harmonica tightly by her chest and waited. A few strums from Mike and Peter and a high note from Audrey at the keyboard, and Amy got ready.

When she got her que from Audrey, she began to play. What came out was mostly sputtering. The timing was way off. The notes she played had no resemblance to the song.

We all looked at each other with no clue of what to do.

Suddenly, Amy just ran out of the garage.

Sammy chased after her and caught up with her in the driveway. We all raced over to the garage door and just stood silent, watching Sammy with Amy.

He reached for her hand. "Where ya goin'? We don't practice without you, Amy. Come back in. OK? You don't have to play your harmonica if you don't want to."

She looked up at Sammy with the saddest eyes.

"I do want toooooo plaaaay. I do...but...I'm afraid I will spoil the muuusssic..."

Sammy held on to her hand. "Listen, Amy, all of us are nervous and afraid too, honest, we are. And you know what, Peter is scared stiff of performing that last song. He has never sung in front of people before, and he's just as up tight as you. Come back and give it another try. OK? Whatcha say? Please say yes."

She gave Sammy a hug and her wide smile returned.

"OK...I'llllll try it aa gain."

When Faces saw Sammy and Amy coming back to the garage, they all ran to their instruments like nothing happened. Amy walked in with her usual big smile and waving her hands like always. She took out her harmonica and looked over to Audrey, waiting for the signal to begin. She began to play. She gave it her very best.

The day of September 19th had arrived. Faces in Time all met at 3:30 at King's Table Restaurant.

On the small stage which was closed off with curtains, Peter was setting up his electric guitar and checking out the sound system. Audrey connected her keyboard. I was busy, too, positioning my drum set. Mike was strumming quietly and tuning his guitar.

I took a little peak through the curtains and saw everyone slowly walking in and looking for their table. All of our parents were invited, including Amy's. About 150 or so guests. As I walked back towards my drum set. I wondered about how Faces was feeling. I knew how nervous I was, but I remembered what my dad told me, "You're not professionals, so don't take it seriously. Just do your best. Have fun at it."

The manager of King's Table, Dennis Langley, came over to greet us. "Hi...Is everything all good here?" he asked.

Our agent, Tommy, answered him.

"Yes, thanks...it's fine...stage is just big enough."

"Great, if there's anything you need, just ask me. You are set to go on right before dinner, at 5:00...OK?"

"Sure, that's fine...We'll be ready...Can we do one last number right after dinner?" Tommy asked. Mr. Langley was not expecting another song.

"Well, that will be an extra treat for the crowd. Sure, go ahead if you like. Good luck Faces," he added nicely.

   Dennis Langley stood at the mike when the curtains were drawn at exactly 5:00 p.m. He opened with an introduction.

   "Good evening, ladies and gentlemen. Welcome to King's Table. I hope you have a wonderful time along with a great meal. I would like to congratulate Harold and Margaret McLauglin on their 15th wedding anniversary." Everyone applauded. He then told a few short marriage jokes and the crowd laughed and clapped. And then, "And now I would like to introduce a new, young group called FACES IN TIME." He moved his arm out wide towards us as he left the stage. When the clapping stopped, we began our first piece. Peter and Audrey started it off. Mike and I joined after one bar. The Best Is Yet To Come was played without a hitch. That gave us a big boost of confidence. The acoustics in the room was just right. After the applause, we went into the second number, This Will Be...I gave a light four taps for the tempo on my tenor drum and we began.

   Audrey had a small solo part and she went at it perfectly. Mike and Peter not only strummed away, but started to swing their hips and move the guitars like Elvis Presley! It was wild! The crowd enjoyed it and gave us a loud applause. We all bowed gracefully and by this time we were full of confidence and couldn't wait to play again...

We started our third number, Through the Years. That too was a blast. Slow, easy and the words were just right for a Wedding Anniversary. What was really cools, the crowd was swaying in the seats, back and forth…lovin' it. Some of them were singin' along with us. It was great!

At its end, Dennis Langley came out to the mike.

"Well, how about that, folks. Let's give another shout out for FACES IN TIME. They will be back for another song after dinner. Thank you Faces for a wonderful musical performance."

When we got to the back of the stage and out of sight, all our parents were there. Lots of hugs and kisses and kudos.

Dinner was being served. Minestrone soup. Then your choice of steak, haddock or lobster or plain ol' mac n cheese. It was an impressive, delicious serving and enjoyed by all.

It was time for our final song.

The curtain was once again pulled back and Dennis stood in front of the mike. "Ladies and gentlemen, I sincerely hope you enjoyed the King's Table dinner. At least as much as I did." He got a big laugh. "I have a special treat for you, including dessert, of course."

"FACES IN TIME will perform a final number for you. Let's give them a big hand...Here they are...FACES IN TIME."

We were set up and ready. I gave two light taps on my drum. That was the signal for Amy. She rose from her chair next to Audrey and walked to the mike, waving her arms to the crowd and giving that big, wonderful smile like she always did. She looked so sweet. Sammy dressed her with a pink T-shirt with our Faces emblem on it, a sky-blue jacket, a pair of black slacks, and a lovely pink cap with a smiley face on the brim. The people clapped and whistled and cheered. And then, Amy reached into her cute little pink purse and took out her shiny new harmonica. She turned to Audrey.

Audrey began the intro and pointed.

Amy began her part in the song, Everything I Do, I Do It For You. She was right on! Never missed a beat! In perfect pitch and key. Amazing! After two bars, she stopped and waved like crazy to the crowd. Peter then walked to the Mike with his guitar and stood aside of Amy. He began to sing.

"LOOK INTO MY EYES...YOU WILL SEE...ALL YOU MEAN TO ME...SEARCH YOUR SOUL... SEARCH NO MORE...
TELL ME WHAT WERE SEARCHING FOR... IT'S TRUE...
EVERYTHING I DO...I DO IT FOR YOU..."

At that part of the song, Amy lifted her harmonica and played along while Peter finished the song...
I DO IT FOR YOOOOUUUUU...

Peter put his arm around Amy and kissed her on the cheek.
Amy waved more and more, like she always did.

Mike and Audrey and I got up and stood right behind Peter and Amy and we all took a bow as the curtain began to close. The crowd clapped loudly and to our surprise, we got a standing ovation. It was a night we will never, ever, forget.

Later that week, Audrey called me and asked to come over and meet in the garage.

She arrived with Amy and another boy. Of course, Amy came in waving and smiling.

"Jack, this is Anthony, Amy's friend."

"Hi, Anthony," I said.

Anthony had the same problem as Amy with speech. He stuttered too. "Nii ccce to mmmeeet you," he replied.

Amy then tugged at my sleeve.

"Tony pppplaays the accorrrr dddion, Jaaaccck," she said. "We play musicccc togethhheeer."

"Wow, Amy, that's terrific!" I answered, looking over at Audrey and wondering what this was all about.

"Will you sssshhowww us how to start a band with the harmonnnniccca and Tony's accordiooonnn, Jack?" she asked with a great big smile.

I looked over at Audrey to see her shrug her shoulders in an I don't know gesture.

"Harmonica and accordion, Amy? Well, I don't know. It sounds interesting and very different. Let me and Faces give it some thought. If we can help, we sure will." Amy gave me her winning smile and big wave as she left with her friend Tony and Audrey.

I sat in my mom's old, dusty lawn chair and thought about Amy. Wow! Harmonica and accordion... Wow!

THE END